SOCIAL (MEDIA) LIFE

MARK ALLAN GUNNELLS

PUBLICATIONS

SOCIAL (MEDIA) LIFE

MARK ALAN GUNNELS

LVP

Lycan Valley Press Publications
1002 N Meridian STE 100-153
Puyallup, Washington 98404 United States of America

Printed in the United States of America

First Edition

ISBN-13: 978-1-64562-023-5

This book is dedicated to my husband and best friend, Craig Metcalf. You have always seen the real me and offered nothing but acceptance and encouragement. I love you always.

SOCIAL (MEDIA) LIFE

Alex sat on his bed, scrolling through pictures on Instagram. He had English Lit reading to do, five chapters to get through before class tomorrow, but he felt unmotivated to go grab his *Norton Anthology* so continued to peruse through photos of people having more fun than Alex ever had in his life.

When his roommate Xavier came into the dorm room, Alex quickly slid his phone underneath his pillow, as if hiding away porn.

"Hey," Alex said. "Haven't seen you all day."

Xavier gave him a skeptical look as he peeled off his shirt. "Well, that's what happens when a person has a life. Their dorm room becomes a place only for the three S's."

"Three S's?"

"Yeah, a place to shit, shower, and sleep. Now if you'll excuse me, I have to do the first two. Me and some of the guys from the lacrosse team are going out tonight."

Alex didn't expect an invitation to join them, but he still felt disappointed when Xavier disappeared into the bathroom and closed the door. The action felt metaphoric as well as literal. Another door closed on Alex.

Retrieving his phone, he pulled up Xavier's Instagram. The account was private so Alex couldn't see any of the photos. At the very start of the semester Alex had requested to follow Xavier, but the request had never been approved. Alex couldn't work up the nerve to ask why.

Mostly because he knew why. Xavier was cool and confident, Alex was awkward and perpetually unsure of himself. Those two personality types were like oil and water; they simply did not mix.

Alex went to his own account. He had only twenty-two followers, most of them family. It didn't really matter as he had made fewer posts than he had followers. Social media was an exhibitionist's dream, but that hinged on having voyeur's eyes watching. A symbiotic relationship. When one lacked the latter, the former seemed pointless.

Dr. McAbee, Alex's art professor, had inquired why he didn't share his drawings on social media. Alex did love to draw, and false modesty aside he had to admit he thought he was pretty good at it. The few family members he'd shown his art to had agreed, his parents not even balking at his decision to major in Art in college as they seemed to recognize his talent and passion. *It's the only thing the boy is good at,* he'd overheard his father telling someone on the phone, his voice a combination of equal parts pride and disappointment.

But his drawing had always felt more private, something that brought him a great deal of joy but which he hesitated to share with other people. Despite believing he did have skill, he nonetheless feared that his artistic flair would provide those around him with yet another reason to ridicule him. He didn't think he'd be able to deal with his one source of joy being tainted that way.

Dr. McAbee, however, seemed to think his art could be the thing that drew people to him. *People are attracted to talent,* she'd said. That seemed too simple to Alex, but he wanted to believe it. That people would see his drawings and suddenly find him more interesting and want to talk to him.

And yet on some level that frightened Alex more than anything. If people wanted to talk to him they would expect him to talk back, and conversation wasn't his forte. His tongue stayed in a perpetual knot.

Alex heard the toilet flush in the bathroom then the shower running. He imagined his roommate out with his friends, laughing easily and having a good time. Alex wanted to be a part of that, friends and camaraderie and feeling like he belonged.

When Xavier came out of the bathroom with only a towel wrapped loosely around his waist, the sight of his athletic and graceful body caused Alex to blush. His own body seemed so clunky and ungainly by comparison. With seemingly no self-consciousness, Xavier dropped the towel and quickly threw on some jeans and a T-shirt, stepping into sneakers before leaving without so much as a goodbye.

Feeling a determination rare for him, Alex climbed off the bed and went to his desk in the corner. He ignored his textbooks and booted up his laptop. He had a locked file that contained scans of most of his drawings. He selected a few he thought were his best then opened Instagram on the computer. He started to upload the drawings but then hesitated. People like Xavier, people who already knew him, wouldn't even look at his artwork. He might be able to get a following of strangers but not the attention of those around him.

Not the attention of Xavier.

Without giving himself too much time to think it over, Alex went into his settings and scrolled down to ADD ACCOUNT. For his username he selected COLLEGE.BOY.ARTIST and for his real name put Xander. Not exactly a lie, sometimes guys named Alexander went by Xander instead of Alex.

For his profile picture, he didn't want to put his own face. That wasn't likely to attract anyone. Instead he went back to his drawings, wanting to use a sample of his work to entice. He found one he'd done last year called "Ideal." It had been an experiment, taking features from different men—

mostly celebrities—and putting them together in an amalgamation so that he Frankensteined together the perfect man. On paper at least.

Once this was done, he uploaded five more of his best drawings. For his profile bio, he decided to go short and sweet.

> College student who loves to draw.
> Likely won't ever make a living at it, but
> it is the only thing I'm good at.

Alex was tempted to go immediately to Xavier's profile and send a follow request, but he figured a strange account with no followers would not be interesting. So first he searched until he found some accounts dedicated to artwork and drawing, and even a few focused on college life, and he followed those, hoping that at least some of the people in those communities would follow him back.

All of this was probably stupid and pointless, but what did he have to lose? After closing the laptop, he finally grabbed the *Norton Anthology* and resigned himself to an evening with Emily Dickinson.

It wasn't until late the next morning after American History that Alex thought to check the new Instagram account. He was delighted but also surprised to see that Xander had in fact garnered some follows overnight. Eleven, in fact. In just one night the new account had gotten almost as many followers as his old one had gotten after several years.

After taking a seat on a bench just outside the library, Alex quickly followed back some of his new followers, noticing many of them were artists themselves. He'd received several likes on his posts and even a few comments complimenting his work. He saw he'd also gotten a private message.

Expecting it to be spam, some sexy single woman who wanted him to be her friend and give his honest reaction to her nudes, he instead discovered a message from the person who ran a page called BleedingArt asking if she could post some of his drawings to the account, giving him credit of course. He didn't answer right away, still struggling with the fear of ridicule and rejection. However, the little bit of affirmation he had received after just one night had bolstered his confidence and he had a feeling it could become addictive. He shot off a quick message telling her he would be honored for her to share his artwork.

He had an hour before English Lit. He'd planned to spend it in the library finishing the Dickinson assignment. He'd made a valiant effort to get through all the assigned poems last night but had ended up bingeing some reality show about glass blowing on his phone instead.

However, when he got up from the bench he turned away from the library and instead hurried back across the quad toward the dorms. He wanted to put up more of his drawings on the new Instagram.

By the end of the week, the new account had almost a hundred followers. BleedingArt had featured several more of his pieces, as well as a page called HomoErectusArt sharing a handful of his more risqué drawings. The likes and compliments came fast and furious, more acceptance than Alex had ever felt in his life.

Riding that high, Alex decided to take a chance.

It was Friday night, and like most Friday nights, Xavier sat at his desk furiously doing his homework. He liked to get it all done right away so he could have the full weekend to enjoy. Alex sat on his bed, scrolling through the Xander Instagram. He hadn't looked at his original one all week. Looking up, studying the way Xavier's forehead wrinkled and he chewed on his bottom lip when concentrating, Alex said, "Wanna go see a movie or something tonight?"

At first Xavier didn't respond or even look at Alex, but his entire body froze. His fingers stilled on the keyboard, his posture stiffened, making him look like a mannequin posed at the desk to sell school supplies. Slowly, like something out of an old *Twilight Zone* episode, the mannequin turned its head in Alex's direction and uttered a single, incredulous word: "What?"

Alex tried to play it cool though he felt himself

shaking like he was out in the cold without a jacket. "Um, I was thinking of going to see the new horror movie that just came out. Figured if you weren't doing anything maybe you'd want to come with."

Xavier looked at Alex as if Alex had just asked him if he wanted to jump from the top of the campus bell tower. "I've got plans tonight, but thanks," he said then turned back to his laptop.

"What kind of plans?"

Without glancing away from the screen, Xavier said, "If you must know, some guys from my Music Appreciation class are in a local band that will be performing at the park downtown."

"That sounds fun," Alex said, knowing that he should stop talking before further humiliation but unable to keep the words from pouring from his mouth like vomit. "What time does the performance start?"

It seemed as if Xavier was going to ignore the question, but then he heaved a dramatic sigh and closed the laptop. Swiveling in his chair to face Alex, he said, "Okay, maybe it's time you and me had a little chat."

Alex barely stopped himself from automatically correcting *you and me* to *you and I*, even as dread settled in his stomach like a lump of molded bread. The prospect of finally having his roommate's attention was something he'd longed for, but the expression on Xavier's face suggested this wasn't going to be a pleasant chat.

"I don't have anything particular against you," Xavier said. "As far as roommates go, you're quiet and give me my space, *usually*. I just don't want you to get the idea that we're going to be more than roommates. We run in different circles. We don't have anything in common."

"We don't even know each other, so how do you know if we have anything in common?"

"Trust me, we don't."

Alex didn't know how to respond to that, so he merely sat on his bed, fighting an internal battle not to let the tears he felt wanting to fall actually materialize.

Xavier stood up, stowing his laptop in a backpack and slinging it over his shoulder. "I'm going to finish my homework in the library."

Alex sat alone in the room for several minutes, still not giving himself permission to cry. His feelings were hurt, yes, but he also felt angry. To be dismissed so out of hand. *We run in different circles.*

Not even true. Xavier ran in circles; Alex was a single dot all unto himself.

Except that wasn't true, either. Not anymore. He had a lot of followers and admirers online, under the new Instagram account.

Alex grabbed his phone and quickly looked up Xavier's account and sent a follow request from Xander. He couldn't say he had anything as solid as a plan, but a vague notion emerged that if Xavier could see his artwork, could see how much people loved it, then maybe it would change his roommate's perception of him.

Of course, he also knew this was at least a little bit dishonest. Xavier wouldn't know the follow request was from Alex, but he had to get his foot in the door somehow. Then he'd reveal who he was and maybe a friendship could start to develop.

That was all Alex wanted.

Or so he told himself.

A few days passed, and Alex had started to think Xavier was going to ignore this follow request as well. Then on Tuesday morning he woke up to find his roommate had accepted and even followed back. Xavier had still been up when Alex went to bed the night before, but now he was buried under his covers and snoring loudly. Alex got out of bed and locked himself in the bathroom.

Not only had Xavier accepted the follow request from the Xander account, he had followed it back and liked all of the posts. He'd commented on three of them. The drawing of an empty beach with only one figure visible in the distance as nothing more than a silhouette:

Very evocative

The one of a young boy and girl sitting on a bench, both licking an ice cream cone held by the girl:

> This one is kind of sweet, almost
> tells a whole story.

And the risqué drawing of a man seen from behind, wearing only a jockstrap, glancing over his shoulder, an image Alex cribbed from a porn he'd watched: the comment on this one was merely a string of the fire emoji.

Alex liked all the comments and chose to respond to the one on the ice cream drawing. He thought about it for several minutes, started typing then deleting, before settling on:

> I guess I wanted to say something
> about generosity and sharing
> without being all preachy.

Sitting on the closed toilet lid, Alex opened Xavier's account, feeling like he'd finally received the key to a locked door he'd been trying to get through for some time. Of course, he'd gotten the key under a false pretense so did that make it stealing? Did that make him a trespasser and voyeur?

Stop being so melodramatic, he told himself. *It's not like you broke into someone's home to watch him sleeping. You're just looking at pictures on a popular social media site.*

It turned out that Xavier posted a lot. There were a ton of selfies, sometimes alone, sometimes with friends. Pictures of meals from various restaurants and even the dining hall, *food porn* as Alex had heard it referred to. Various shots from around campus: the bell tower at sunset, the fountain behind the library, ducks swimming across the lake next to the bookstore. The photos dated all the way back to a younger Xavier in high school.

Alex was tempted to just go through all of them hitting the little heart icon, but he didn't want to seem like a lunatic. Sure, Alex had liked all of his posts but those only totaled to thirteen. Over the years, Xavier's account had accumulated maybe a hundred photos. Forcing himself to be cool, Alex went through and liked a handful of the most recent ones. He chose to make only one comment, on a selfie of Xavier at a mountain lookout, a panoramic view laid out behind him. Alex's comment was a single word.

Beautiful

Of course, he could have been referring to the view or to Xavier's face lit up with the kind of smile he never turned on Alex, but the ambiguity of the comment was part of its perfection.

Alex nearly dropped the phone when someone pounded on the bathroom door. Not from Alex and Xavier's side, but the dorm room next door that shared this bathroom. "You done in there?" said one of the suitemates. "I gotta take a piss."

Flushing the toilet as a cover, Alex unlocked both doors then scurried back into his room. Xavier was still asleep, flat on his stomach with his head turned to the side, one arm dangling over the side of the bed. Alex stood for a moment, watching his roommate's back rise and fall with each breath, but then he turned away, not wanting to feel like a creeper.

Even if he was one.

Later that morning in English Lit, Dr. Carver droning on about the possible relationship between Emily Dickinson and a Presbyterian minister named Charles Wadsworth, Alex's cell began vibrating in his pocket. He didn't hesitate to pull it out and check the notification. He sat in the very back of the classroom, and besides, he had found that college was a lot more laidback than high school.

Xavier had responded to Alex's response on the ice cream drawing.

> I love that through your art you're a storyteller. I sometimes write poems myself so I know that urge to tell a story.

Alex was stunned. He had no idea his roommate dabbled in poetry. There was so much Alex didn't know, so many layers not yet unraveled. And he wanted to unravel those layers and get tangled up in them.

I'd love to read something of yours

Alex responded then regretted after hitting the POST button. Maybe it was too familiar too fast. He didn't exactly have much in the way of social skills so he often floundered at the most basic of interactions. It was too late to take it back now. All he could do was wait to see if Xavier responded.

Xavier didn't respond directly to Alex's comment, but he did respond in a much more public way. That afternoon Alex found the Xander account tagged in a new post from Xavier.

> My friend @College.Boy.Artist suggested I should share some of my writing. That's right, folks, I write too. So here's a little sampling. Don't laugh at me too hard, my ego is delicate.

Below this was a screenshot of a short poem. Sitting on a bench in the rose garden, Alex read the poem several times. It suggested a depth to Xavier, a longing for connectedness, that most would not suspect in a popular jock.

> You don't know me,
> But you think you do.
> You see the image I project
> Without ever looking beyond the surface.
> I am perhaps as much to blame
> As anyone else for my invisibility.
> Maybe the time has come
> To turn the projector off
> And let the charade fall away.
> You don't know me,

But maybe you will.

Alex hit the heart icon and commented.

> **This is beautiful. You use words to create imagery the way I use pencil and ink.**

Alex was surprised when he got a response from Xavier within less than a minute.

> **Thank you. Honestly I am very nervous, no one knows I'm a wannabe poet. I hope I haven't embarrassed myself too bad.**

Alex typed back.

> **Not at all. I mean it when I say it's beautiful. Certainly makes me want to get to know you more.**

More regret, wondering if he'd said too much. Then the quick response:

> **Same here. I think we probably have a lot in common and would get along really well.**

Alex's cheeks ached, and only then did he realize he was grinning like an idiot. He had broken through Xavier's wall. Sure, he had been forced to project a charade of his own to do it, but now that Xavier was starting to see that he and Alex weren't really that different perhaps Alex could come clean.

But how to do that without leaving Xavier feeling as if he'd been tricked and manipulated? That was going to be the challenge.

On Thursday, Alex finished his latest drawing. This one was another version of his "Ideal" creation, a semi-nude with the guy sitting on the edge of a bed in only his underwear, leaned forward with his elbows on his knees. Alex saw it as a homage of sorts to Rodin's *The Thinker*. Alex uploaded it to Instagram and captioned it,:

Early Morning Contemplations

That afternoon, as he sat at a table by himself in the dining hall—the DH as most of the other students called it—he got a notification that Xavier had liked the new post, but also that Xavier had sent him a private message.

Alex put the phone down on the table and slid it away from himself. His breathing sounded loud in his own ears, and he felt sweat begin to form around his hairline. He knew he was being absurd. It was just a message, and they'd already replied to each other's comments. But this felt different, more intimate. It was a *private* message, after all.

Finally he grabbed his phone again and opened the message. He read it, then reread it, then read it again.

> Hey there, X-man! Hope you don't mind if I call you that. My dad sometimes calls me that and since both our names start with an X we

could be the X-men. LOL Anyway I just want to say how much I have been enjoying your artwork. It's so detailed and evocative. I get it now when they say a picture is worth a thousand words. I won't lie the erotic stuff is also just a pleasure to look at. And since I'm already going there I have to say that you're hot as hell. Hope that wasn't too forward but there it is."

It was the last bit that had Alex so confused. *Hot as hell*, he said. But that didn't make any sense. Xavier gave no indication he had figured out that Xander was really Alex, not that he thought Xavier would ever describe him as hot as hell anyway. So what made Xavier think he knew what Xander looked like? Alex had never posted anything but his drawings.

"Oh shit," Alex said under his breath, but still loud enough that some girls at a nearby table glanced his way then laughed. He didn't pay them any attention because he thought he was starting to figure this out.

The latest post was a variation on the same "Ideal" character that served as the profile picture for the Xander Twitter account. So Xavier...

"He thinks it's a self-portrait," Alex murmured.

That hadn't been Alex's intent, not at all. He had made "Ideal" the profile photo only because he thought it was his best work and he wanted to spotlight it in a way. But with the addition of a new piece with the same face, naturally Xavier would assume he was drawing himself. Now that it had happened, Alex could see how inevitable it was.

There's a word for this, Alex thought. *Catfishing.*

Again Alex told himself that hadn't been his intention, and yet hadn't it? At least a little bit? He was purposely hiding who he was and while telling no active lies, he had engaged Xavier knowing that his roommate had no idea of his real identity. Sure, he'd figured eventually he would reveal the truth, harboring the fantasy that he and Xavier would then become fast friends if not more. Ignoring the fact that such a revelation would probably lead to feelings of betrayal and anger. He had thought of this as a charade, a masquerade, when really at its core this was nothing more than deception.

And now here Alex was, in quite the mess. If Alex was going to tell Xavier the truth, now was the time. Tell the truth and face the consequences. Either that or just deactivate the Xander account and disappear. Ghosting rather than catfishing.

With trembling hands, Alex quickly typed out a message. Thumb hovering over the SEND button, he read back over his message.

Thanks, you're pretty hot yourself.

Then he hit SEND.

Alex spent the next few hours regretting his rash decision to bolster Xavier's misconception instead of correct it. Of course, he didn't regret it enough to do anything to rectify it. He took the more passive approach of what's done is done and now he would sit back and see how it all played out.

As afternoon turned to evening and he'd received no response from Xavier, he started to worry that he had gone too far by saying he was hot. Yet that didn't make sense, as he had only been reciprocating in kind after Xavier called him hot. Or called Xander hot at least. So perhaps Xavier was hurt that he'd sent a longer message and received a short one line response in return. Or maybe…

Walking down the hall toward his dorm room, Alex suddenly paused as a darker possibility occurred to him. What if Xavier had in fact figured out that the Xander account was Alex and the message had been a test to see if his roommate would come clean? A test that Alex had failed.

Alex stood in the hallway for a moment, suddenly dreading going into his room in case Xavier was there and ready to confront him. Only when a door opened behind him did Alex hurry on and let himself into his room.

He found Xavier lying on his bed, staring down at his phone. He glanced up briefly when Alex walked in, but his expression didn't evince anger or rage. If anything, only mild annoyance. He turned back to his phone without so much as a hello.

Alex crossed the room, un-shouldering his pack and slinging it over the back of his desk chair. He was surprised to discover that underneath the relief he also felt a bit of disappointment that Xavier hadn't figured it out. He realized a part of him had harbored the fantasy that Xavier would say he knew that Alex was Xander but that Alex didn't have to hide behind a fake online persona. Xavier would apologize for being so cold and unfriendly, Alex would be magnanimous and say he understood, they would shake hands which would lead to a hug which may lead to more…

Of course, Alex realized such a scenario was so unrealistic it might as well be classified as bizarro fiction. Yet even if his worst fear had come true, Xavier had figured it out and wanted to yell and accuse and even punch, at least then it would be over. Alex seemed too cowardly to end the charade himself, so the idea of it being exposed in a way that was out of his hands held a certain allure.

Alex sat at his desk, booting up his laptop with the vague intention of starting on the paper he had due for Intro to Psych. However, he couldn't concentrate, and other than the header the page remained white and blank. It was too quiet in the room, nothing but the sound behind him of Xavier's fingers tapping on his phone screen. He still hadn't responded to Xander's last message, so who was he messaging? Alex felt a surge of jealousy rise up in him like bile. He realized that was absurd, but there it was nonetheless.

"How was your day?" Alex finally asked, just to fill the silence. He didn't turn around, but he could faintly see his roommate's reflection in the laptop screen.

"It was a day."

"Nothing interesting happened?"

"Do you mind?" Xavier said, his voice sharp as shattered glass. "I'm in the middle of something here."

Now Alex did turn around, throwing an arm over the back of the chair. "In the middle of what?"

With a groan, Xavier rolled off his bed and put on his shoes. "I'm going to the library."

After Xavier left, Alex abandoned all pretense that he was going to start his paper, instead balling up on his bed to sulk. Why couldn't he get Xavier to talk to him? What was it about Alex that was so repugnant that it repelled his roommate? It could only be his looks, because Xavier didn't seem to have that same reaction to Xander and except for appearance, Xander and Alex were the same person.

Only now Xavier had stopped talking to Xander as well. So perhaps it wasn't just about looks. Maybe too much of Alex's personality had seeped through in the social media exchanges and that was what sent Xavier running.

Alex slapped himself, lightly at first, but then another time with force, tears leaking from his eyes.

"Stupid, stupid, stupid," he said like a mantra. He pulled at his hair and slapped himself a few more times, a self-flagellation that had become a part of his normal routine in high school. Not to mention the healing cut marks on his thighs. However, he had promised himself that college would be a new day, the flipping to a new page, turning over of a new leaf, a journey of self-discovery and reinvention.

And yet here he was, beating up on himself again both figuratively and literally. The temptation to lock himself in the bathroom with a pair of scissors was strong, but instead he cried himself into a stupor, a semi-doze. He wasn't sure how long this lasted, but the vibration of his phone roused him.

When he glanced at the screen and saw the notification for a new message from Xavier, Alex at first wondered if he'd fallen asleep and slipped into some kind of wish-fulfillment dream. However, the dried snot on his upper lip and the desperate need to urinate suggested this was plain old reality. He pushed up and opened the message.

> Hey X-Man. First off let me apologize for taking so long to respond. I know this will sound silly but I started many responses and then deleted them. All day I've been trying to compose the perfect message and rejecting my efforts for various reasons. This one sounded too formal, that one sounded too

flippant, too saccharine, too suggestive. So I decided to stop trying to compose and just talk, like if we were sitting together at a table sharing a coffee or something. And I've made the vow that I'm sending this message no matter what. So here goes.

I like you. May sound ridiculous as I don't really know you, but I'm not professing my undying love or asking for your hand or anything. I'm just saying I like you, enough that I want to get to know you better. And I want you to get to know me better. Not a lot of people know me, not really. I mean, you might be able to tell from some of my photos on here that I'm a jock, and yeah, I love sports, always have. But I'm also a poet which you know. Not everyone gets that those two things can co-exist in one person. Seems like you do. Might be nice to have a friend that I feel really gets me. If you want to be my friend, that is. Don't want to be presumptuous. Okay, now I'll sit around and wait, chewing my nails off, hoping that I haven't totally embarrassed myself here. If I don't hear back from you, I'll know I have, but I hope I haven't. I hope you want to be friends."

Even as Alex finished reading the message, a second one came through. Just two sentences this time:

> P.S. Just out of curiosity what college do you go to? Your bio doesn't say.

For a moment, Alex could only sit there, feeling a bit dazed. He had spent all day stressing over getting a response from Xavier, and it turned out Xavier had spent all day stressing over sending the response. And now was stressing over whether or not Alex would respond.

Correction, whether or not *Xander* would respond.

In any case, it had never occurred to Alex that someone as popular and gorgeous as Xavier could be insecure, could feel isolated even in a crowd. His message was full of vulnerability and truth, full of a certain loneliness Alex could relate to, a tentative reaching out of his hand, hoping someone would take it instead of slapping it away.

This left Alex reeling with a confusion of emotions. He felt elated, of course, honored that Xavier felt he could open up and show his true self, but he also felt a crushing sense of guilt because while Xavier offered up honesty, all Alex offered up was deception. This whole thing may not have started as a catfishing scheme, but that was unquestionably what it was in danger of becoming.

Unless he stopped it now.

But how could he stop it now? If he told the truth right after Xavier had started to pour his heart out, it could only result in a rage. And possibly worse. Could Alex get into serious trouble for this ruse? If not legally, with the college? Best case scenario, he'd be forced to switch rooms, but worst case scenario he'd be expelled from school.

No, the smart thing to do would be to end it. Xavier had expressed the fear that Xander wouldn't respond, that he would be put off by Xavier's heartfelt message, so Alex could manifest that.

Yet that seemed so unfair to Xavier. It wasn't his fault that Alex had started this, and such a rejection could crush the young man, make him feel like he could never show his true self to anyone. He'd potentially burrow even deeper into his shell, build a protective armor around himself. That might sound melodramatic to some, but not to anyone who had ever faced serious rejection.

As Alex himself had.

Maybe somehow Xavier and Xander could maintain their friendship. Xander wasn't real, true, but Xavier didn't know that and didn't have to know that. They could remain as they were, online friends. That way Alex would get to vicariously be a part of his roommate's life in a way he wasn't on a day-to-day, face-to-face basis, and Xavier would get the chance to open up and truly be himself with someone. A win/win.

A part of Alex's brain knew this was a terrible

idea, setting up for nothing but disaster, but that part was shouted down by a need to connect, even if through a made-up persona.

Alex thought for a moment of what school to say Xander attended. He was tempted to pick somewhere on the West Coast, as far as he could get and still be in the country, but then he hesitated. If it was too far, might that make Xavier lose interest and the friendship fizzle out because Xander seemed too unobtainable?

So somewhere closer, but not too close. Close enough that it seemed possible, but far enough that it would be impractical.

In the end, Alex chose a college two states away.

Alex dreamt he was fly fishing. Odd since in real life Alex had never been fishing in his life. Then again, in dreams people could do all sorts of things they never did in real life. For some that meant in dreams they could fly, but for Alex it was fishing.

He stood in the middle of a large river, the water rushing past him, like in this old Robert Redford movie he'd watched with his mother once. The day was overcast, but the clouds were not dark with rain but neither were they white. Instead they were a neon green that pulsed and flared as if some alien craft hovered inside them. This didn't strike Alex as weird. Nothing in a dream ever seemed weird in the thick of it. In fact, in the distance on the far side of the lake he saw a brontosaurus lumbering by, stopping to eat leaves off the top-

most branches of nearby trees. Alex noted this with a shrug and sent his fishing line sailing out into the water with a flick of his wrist.

After some time he became aware that he was not alone. Standing off to his side was Xavier, with his own fishing pole. The man wore his lacrosse jersey and a jockstrap only. His expression was stony with seriousness, watching the spot where his line sank into the water.

"I didn't know you liked to fish," Alex said.

Xavier didn't respond, didn't in any way acknowledge that Alex was there. He seemed so still and so focused that he might as well have been a statue out here in the river.

Thinking maybe he hadn't been heard, Alex tried again. "It's a nice day to be out, isn't it?"

Finally Xavier looked at him. He didn't turn his head but merely cut his eyes in Alex's direction. "Do you mind? I'm in the middle of something here."

"Oh, sorry," Alex said, feeling chastised. "I didn't mean to distract you."

"You're not a distraction. I'd have to know you existed to find you distracting."

The words stung Alex like a pelting of pebbles. He wondered if he should go back to the shore, maybe find a different spot further down the river. Xavier likely wouldn't even notice.

Alex was about to pull in his line when Xavier cried out and the other man's line started to play out, the reel spinning. "I got something!" Xavier shouted gleefully. "I actually got a bite!"

Alex watched, a vicarious thrill coursing through his body, holding his breath as Xavier cranked the handle, trying to reel in the fish. Whatever he'd caught must have been big and strong because it fought against the line. At one point, the pole was nearly yanked right out of Xavier's hands, and he nearly fell over into the water, fighting to keep his balance. The clouds above turned from green to an ominous red, a bloody sky closing over the top of the scene.

As Xavier screamed through gritted teeth, continuing to reel the fish in little by little, Alex wondered if he should offer his help, but he felt frozen in place. Besides, he couldn't imagine a scenario where Xavier would accept his help. So he merely watched, always the voyeur of life, saying a silent prayer and cheer, wanting to see Xavier get what he wanted, to get the prize. If Alex was present for this triumph, even if he didn't help facilitate it, maybe that would cause Xavier to see him in a more favorable light.

Maybe.

Finally, with a primal scream, Xavier tugged on the pole and the fish came splashing out of the water as if propelled by a cannon, flying through the air in an arc, seeming to defy the very laws of gravity. Xavier tossed his pole aside and held out his hands like a football player preparing to catch a pass, and the fish landed right in his arms, cradled like a baby.

The fish was huge, gray and scaly with a floppy dorsal fin on its back and ropy whiskers. A catfish. Xavier had caught a catfish.

Suddenly Alex's perspective in the dream shifted. He was no longer looking over at Xavier but instead looking up at him. Xavier seemed like a giant all of a sudden, his head a planet leaning down toward him. "You're a big fella," Xavier said in the booming voice of a God, a voice like thunder from the clouds that had gone an icy blue. "You gave me a hell of a lot of trouble, but I caught you now."

Alex realized with a numbed horror that he was the catfish, cradled in Xavier's arm. His horror was tempered, however, with knowing this might be the only way he'd get to be in his roommate's arms.

Xavier carried Alex out of the river and back to the shore. Here he dropped Alex onto the sandy, rocky ground. A fall that felt like miles, a skydiver who had jumped out the plane without his parachute. The impact was painful, but not as painful as the lack of oxygen that made Alex feel as if a great weight sat on his scaly little chest, crushing his lungs.

He flopped and wheezed and tried to draw oxygen into his gills, but the air around him was noxious to his system. He was dying, and he knew it.

A great shadow fell over him as the giant Xavier knelt by his side, his lips twisted in a wicked smile. "You're going to make a great meal, my friend."

Then Alex saw the knife in Xavier's hand, swooping down, and Alex was trying to scream when the blade sank into his flesh, cutting off his head—

Alex awoke from this nightmare drenched in sweat and with a scream stuck in his throat like a lump of dried bread. Yet despite how disturbing the dream had been, his covers were tented by the erection underneath.

Over the next month, Xavier and Xander talked

every day. The conversations moved off of Instagram and onto Snapchat, which of course necessitated Alex creating a Snapchat for Xander. They talked about things they liked, shared common interests.

Of course, it turned out Xavier and Alex didn't have a lot of shared common interests. They had vastly different tastes in music—Alex preferred Adele, Xavier liked someone called Yeat—movies— Alex was into horror movies, Xavier raucous comedies—and sports—Alex hated all sports, Xavier loved them all except hockey which he said lacked any grace. Alex was withdrawn and shy, Xavier gregarious and confident.

And yet while Xavier had little in common with Alex, it turned out he had much in common with Xander. Alex felt almost like a writer, or what he imagined a writer would feel like creating a character from whole cloth. He downloaded the music and movies Xavier liked, looked up facts and stats for the sports teams and players his roommate mentioned. He didn't want it to be so obvious, so once he had the information he needed, he used it as a springboard for further research. So instead of saying Xander liked Yeat, for instance, he picked artists that were in a similar vein. Like Ken Car$on and Summrs. That kind of music didn't actually appeal to Alex at all, but Xander loved it.

And Alex started to think of himself and Xander in separate terms. Xander was no longer an alter-ego but a fully distinct entity removed from his origins.

Oddly, the more Xavier and Xander talked, the less Xavier and Alex did. They shared a room but barely acknowledged each other. Xavier seemed preoccupied, always on his phone. Alex, on the other hand, feared he might accidentally mention something Xavier had only told to Xander, a slip that could send this whole house of cards toppling down, so he kept his mouth shut when Xavier was around.

The conversations between Xavier and Xander became progressively more flirtatious but never downright dirty. At least not as of yet. Alex found himself worrying that eventually Xavier would want to see a real photo, not just a drawing, or maybe even have a video chat. So far the possibility hadn't been brought up. In fact, the first mention of a photo came from Xavier in an unexpected way.

> If I send you a pic of me, would you draw it?

Alex was sitting in the café just off the bookstore when he read this message. Xavier didn't know that Alex had already done a few sketches of his roommate, and he didn't want to tell him and scare him off. Instead he replied:

> Sure, I think you'd be a hell of a subject.
> I'll pay you for it, of course.

> Don't be silly. It would be an honor to draw you. Do you have a particular picture in mind?

> Yeah, but I haven't taken it yet. I'll have to wait til I get the room to myself. Seems like my dork-ass roommate is always around.

Alex paused with his coffee halfway to his mouth. The music and the chatter around him suddenly seemed very loud, and he felt as if everyone were pressing in on him. He had never considered himself claustrophobic or agoraphobic, but now sweat beaded around his hairline and his breathing became irregular. He thought for a moment, deciding how he wanted to respond.

> You've never mentioned your roommate before. Is he a real dweeb?

Dweeb? Who the hell used that kind of word but a real dweeb?

> Look I don't want to be mean. In some ways I feel sorry for the guy. He's such a mess and I suspect he has a mad crush on me. It's kind of sad. I've already decided I'm going to petition next semester to change rooms. Let someone else deal with this dweeb. That's a good word for him LOL

Part of Alex felt crushed, a cold pain piercing his chest like a blade of ice, but another part of him felt nothing. The part that was in Xander mode at the moment. That part read the message and had no reaction because it wasn't about him.

Putting down the drink and picking up the phone, he typed out:

Guy sounds pathetic

For the next couple of days, Alex stayed out of the dorm room as much as possible. He spent time at the library, the bookstore café, took the bus into town to wander the park and browse the stores. On one level, he didn't want to be around Xavier now that he knew definitively how his roommate felt about him. On another level, however, he wanted to give Xavier the space and privacy he needed to take the photo for Xander.

Alex was sitting in the rose garden eating lunch on a Saturday when the photo finally came. Upon opening it, Alex started choking on a bite of his chicken sandwich and had to spit it out. His face flushed with heat and he looked around to make sure no one was nearby, no one close enough to see the screen of Alex's phone.

The photo showed Xavier on his bed, the angle from down at his feet and looking up his body. His legs were bent, feet firmly on the mattress, knees spread to expose the rest of him. He wore only a jockstrap—why did Alex suddenly flash on the image of a river and a fish?—the bulge looking almost like a mountain, over which offered a view of his flat stomach and sculpted chest. He had his hands behind his head as if preparing for a sit-up, his face raised slightly to show the hint of a devilish smile.

There was a message with the photo, but Alex didn't notice it yet. The image itself proved quite distracting. When he was finally able to drag his gaze away, he read the text.

> You have no idea how long it took me to get just the right shot. I had to set the phone on my desk and set the timer on the camera. I hope you're not shocked by the scandalous pose but think of it like the scene in that old Titanic movie. Draw me like one of your French girls.

Alex stared at the photo again, crossing his legs to hide the almost painful erection straining at the front of his jeans. He had not asked for a sexy photo, and he hadn't expected one. However, in hindsight he shouldn't have been surprised. This whole situation continued to spiral more and more out of control, and he felt helpless to stop it. Of course, he wasn't helpless. He was merely weak.

He quickly typed out:

> Hot stuff! After a cold shower, I'll get started on the drawing.

As Alex waited for his erection to subside so he

could get up and leave the garden, he thought about Xavier's mention of *Titanic*. Alex himself had never seen that movie so he didn't really get the "French girls" reference, but he did know that the real life story ended in tragedy and death.

An apt metaphor?

Alex had a hard time finding somewhere to do the drawing. He couldn't very well work on the project in his room where Xavier might see, and he couldn't think of anywhere on campus private enough either. He could take the bus into downtown, but usually the streets and the nearby park were packed with pedestrians.

Then Alex remembered the trail that ran along the back of the campus. It was paved over an old railroad line and actually ran for twenty-two miles. He could access the trail on the far side of the lake, and one direction would take him toward downtown and the other toward a small little town with only a few shops and restaurants.

After gathering up his sketchpad and pencils, Alex headed out and got on the trail around ten in the morning, deciding to head away from downtown. The trail itself proved to be a busy little thoroughfare, full of walkers, joggers, bikers, skateboarders. He even saw a family zip by on those ridiculous Segway things, like scooters you stand up on. He was starting to think he'd made a bad choice when up ahead he saw a small path that led off the main one, disappearing into a tree-lined area.

Alex ducked down this branching path, barely avoiding being run down by a cyclist who seemed to think he was competing in the Tour de France, and found himself in a strange little area full of exercise equipment. A sign announced it as a Fitness Park. There was stuff to work your arms, your legs, an exercise bike and an elliptical. And judging by the layer of dust and dried leaves on the equipment, rarely did people use this park. Maybe it said something about America, an abandoned and unused fitness park. Alex even thought it would make an interesting drawing.

Then again, maybe it was all about location. On the trail, people were already getting their exercise. Perhaps it seemed redundant to have a little outdoor gym here.

Whatever the case, Alex felt he had found the perfect place to do his drawing. He found a spot on the pavement by the elliptical, brushed away some old moldering leaves, and had a seat. He pulled up the photo Xavier had sent on his phone, studied it for a few minutes, then opened his pad to a fresh page.

He felt that familiar electrical excitement coursing through him. A fresh page always had this energizing effect on him. A blank page represented possibility and discovery, and he had the power to create worlds out of his mind and hand. It was the only time in his life he felt confident and in control. In fact, when he drew, he often had a bit of a chub in his pants. The act was arousing without being sexual in a way he wasn't sure he could adequately verbalize.

Of course, with the erotic subject matter for this particular drawing, the experience was both arousing and sexual, and Alex's usual chub was a full-on erection as he worked.

At first he half-expected to be interrupted by some buffed exercise freak who jogged over to work on his delts and quads, but no one came. He heard plenty of people continuing to pass by on the other side of the trees, but no one ventured into the Fitness Park.

After a while, Alex relaxed and stopped hearing the passing crowds, no longer felt the pavement underneath him, didn't feel it when a bee landed on the back of his neck and scuttled about before taking off again. He was in the mythic Zone that artists talk about, when the real world drops away and you get lost in your creation. Artists often talked about the Zone as if it were magic, and truthfully it felt a little like that. People who weren't natural creatives often dismissed this kind of talk as hyperbole or pretentiousness, but Alex could attest it was real.

He lost all track of time, and when he first heard the grumbling, he didn't know where the sound originated and he looked around to see if he'd been joined by a raccoon or small dog. Then when the grumbling repeated, he realized his own body was the culprit. His stomach was growling, demanding food. He checked the time on his phone and was surprised to find it was after four in the afternoon. He had skipped breakfast this morning, worked through lunch, and now it was nearly dinner time.

But he had accomplished a lot. The drawing was mostly done. He still had some shading to do, and he wanted to tweak the smile on Xavier's face. He didn't think he had quite captured the devilish charm. Yet overall he thought he'd done a good job and Xavier should be pleased.

You know Xavier doesn't really care about this drawing, don't you? He just wanted an excuse to send Xander a sexy picture, hoping to nudge the relationship into more X-rated territory. He's probably hoping that Xander will reciprocate by sending his own inappropriate photo.

Alex could not deny the truth of any of that, but he couldn't break off the ruse. Not now. And if he were entirely honest with himself, it didn't even feel like a ruse anymore. Yes, he had made Xander up, but in a weird way he felt real to Alex. Again he thought in terms of professional writers who often said their characters felt real to them. Xander definitely was real to Xavier, and it would seem cruel somehow to take that away from his roommate.

So what if they started having dirty and suggestive chats? Xander was still hundreds of miles away, so what could be the harm in them having a little sexy cyber fun?

Even as he gathered up his supplies and headed back for campus, Alex knew the answer.

A lot. The harm could be considerable.

Xavier loved the drawing. He lavished praise on Xander's skill as an artist, and how it turned out even better than he'd imagined.

Things did not turn more overtly sexual after that, however. Alex wasn't sure if he was relieved or disappointed. Things did turn more personal though. Xavier started talking about his family, specifically that his mother knew he was gay but not his father. In fact, his mother had suggested they not tell her husband because she didn't think he would understand. Xavier sometimes wondered if the fact that he was a jock would make it easier for his father to accept or perhaps just confuse him even more. He struggled with having to hide that side of himself from one of the most important people in his life.

Alex made up a family for Xander. A single mother, a father and step-mother he didn't hate, and a younger sister that he had a love/hate relationship with. Unlike Alex's actual family who had no idea about Alex's orientation, Xander's family knew and accepted it. Tentatively at first, but they seemed to be getting more comfortable with it. Tonya, his sister, sometimes referred to him as her fairy god brother but it wasn't done with malice. No different than calling him a dork. Affectionate sibling hazing.

Xavier said he had started coming out to some of his athlete friends and by and large they didn't have a problem with it. A few were a bit standoffish since they found out, but no one had really given him any grief to his face. As with the family, Alex made up a friend group for Xander. Small so as to be realistic, but a group of artistic types who lived and breathed for their passion to create. He joked that Xavier was the first jock friend he'd ever had. Alex thought that was a nice touch.

Things continued on that way for a week until the message from Xavier that sent everything spiraling.

> Hey fellow X-man, our fall break is two weeks away, but I looked up the schedule for your school and saw you have fall break next week. Could I talk you into taking a road trip to visit? I could skip a few classes and really show you around. I think it would be fun.

When Alex initially read the message, he couldn't react. He was sitting at his desk trying to study for the impending midterms while Xavier was reclined on his bed—the same bed where he'd posed for the sexy photo—concentrating on his phone. So Alex had to hide his terror at the prospect. He had thought he'd established Xander far enough away that this wouldn't happen, but he realized now that two states was nothing really. He should have placed Xander in California after all, or even Hawaii, or in Australia for fuck's sake.

Trying to act casual in case Xavier glanced his way, Alex placed the phone on top of his book so he could type out a message without it being obvious he was typing out a message. Thinking quickly, he made his excuses.

> Damn man I'd love that but next week is my grandmother's birthday' 80 years old so a milestone. I can't miss it. I know it sucks and I'm so sorry.

After he sent the message, he heard the soft ding of Xavier's phone behind him, indicating the message had been delivered. He also became hyper aware of the soft sound of the pads of Xavier's fingers tapping on his screen. The message came a minute later.

> That's okay. I mean I'm emotionally devastated even more than I was at the ending of Titanic but I understand. Family has to come first. But maybe I can come up to you during our fall break. Don't answer yet just think about it.

No worries there, Alex thought. He doubted seriously he'd be able to think of anything else.

The next week, Xander didn't message as much. Alex wanted to make it seem he was super busy with his family obligations. He even drew a picture of an older woman blowing out birthday candles on a two-layered cake with the caption HAPPY BIRTHDAY NANA! then posted it on the Xander Instagram account. The amount of work he was doing to keep up this charade bordered on exhausting, and he started to think he had to find an exit ramp before he crashed and burned.

Maybe that was the solution, a car crash. Alex had given birth to Xander; perhaps he could kill him. Make an announcement on his Instagram, say it's from his mother or something, announcing the tragic news.

No, Xavier was already totally invested. He would be online in a heartbeat looking for an obituary, information on a funeral so he could attend. If Alex wanted to extradite himself from the trap he'd made, he would have to find another way out.

After a week of mulling it over, he'd come no closer to finding one.

The Saturday before midterm week, meaning only one more week before fall break and Xavier's desire to visit Xander, a huge party was held in the dorm. Sort of a 'Let's take a break from studying and blow off some steam' kind of a soiree. Alex hadn't been invited, but a dorm party wasn't the kind of thing you needed an invite to get into. There wasn't even a centralized location, but the entire building became a roaming party. Normally Alex would have hid in his own room during the event, but he welcomed the opportunity for a little distraction. Anything to get his mind off his own self-made dilemma.

At first he felt self-conscious as he walked the halls, worrying that everyone would be staring at him and wondering why he thought he could join them in their revelry, but he quickly discovered that no one was paying him any attention. They were all lost in their own world of loud music, loud chatter, loud laughter... all fueled by ample booze.

Technically this was a dry campus, and the RAs were not supposed to allow this kind of debauched party, but the RAs were barely older than the students and a few of them had even provided some of the alcohol. Alex had never had so much as a sip of beer in his life, but when he saw a cooler full of amber glass bottles in the first floor lounge, he decided that now might be a good time to start. If he wanted to obliterate certain thoughts and worries from his mind, what better prescription than his first drunk.

He grabbed a beer out of the ice, the glass freezing his fingers. His first sip made him wince and he had to resist the urge to gag. The brew tasted awful, like a cocktail of piss and sweat and herbal tea. As he took a second pull on the bottle, he wondered how anyone could get addicted to something that tasted so gross.

By the time he finished that first bottle, however, he thought he might be starting to understand. It wasn't about how it tasted, but how it made you *feel*. The world which normally seemed so cruel and bright and hard softened around him, becoming fuzzy around the edges. His head, which usually was full of brittle thoughts like broken glass, instead filled with fizz like the carbonation in a soda. His problems didn't seem so bad suddenly, and he didn't feel so awkward. He found himself talking and laughing with people he didn't even know. Beer was like a bit of magic, he thought, that could turn you into something other than who you really were. And for someone who hated who they really were, that could be powerfully addictive.

By his third beer, Alex thought that the alcohol had another magical quality. Even as it made the world more fuzzy, it clarified certain things. Because it dampened over-thinking, it opened up the mind to simpler solutions.

Finding a quiet oasis in the second floor laundry room, he sat on top of one of the dryers. He knocked over his beer, the remaining contents water-falling to the floor, but he didn't notice. He pulled out his phone to send a message to Xavier. He had to squint at the screen, and his thumbs seemed clumsier than normal, but he had to get it out now. Beer also gave courage of conviction, which even in his tipsy state he suspected would fade when he came down off the high.

> Im sory but I cant Its not a good idea 4 u to come see me during you're brake. This is all going 2 fast and thats partly my fault I no. Its nothing you done but I got out of a relationship only a couple months ago annd I dont think Im ready 4 what I think u want from us. I mean part of me wants it two but I also think if I rush in to it wont be good 4 eithr of us I know its not what u want to here but its better to tell u than lead u on. I care about u2 much for that.

Alex was tempted to read it over, correct all the typos, do some editing, but he feared that would provide too much time for him to change his mind. So as soon as he finished the message, he sent it. It made him feel a little sick, though the beer may have contributed to that, but mostly what he felt was relief. He'd done the right thing, and it had only taken getting slightly drunk to do it. Of course, doing the right thing also meant he had to lose something that had come to mean so much to him.

So in celebration and mourning, he hopped off the dryer, stumbled and kicked the beer bottle out of the way, then went out into the hall for more beer.

All told, Alex had five beers that night. Or maybe it was seven. And a shot of something. He didn't know what, they had been passing them out in a room on the third floor and he took one as he walked by. It was after midnight by the time he made it back to his room. He'd have been there before midnight except in his inebriated state he had trouble finding it.

When he walked inside, kicking the door shut behind him, the room was completely dark but he could hear sounds that it took him a few seconds to identify. Soft, wet sobs and trilling sniffles. Someone was crying.

"Xavier?"

"Leave me alone," Xavier said, his voice muffled which meant he must have had his face in the pillow. "Just go to bed."

Alex reached over and flipped the light switch. The resulting glare was harsh and bright, stabbing into Alex's eyes like an assault. Xavier reacted in a similar fashion, and he quickly pulled the covers up over his head. To hide from the light, but also perhaps to hide his tear-streaked face from his roommate.

"You out of your fucking mind? Turn off the goddamn light, asshole!"

Alex did, the darkness falling back over them like a blessing. He didn't move from the door for a moment, waiting for his bleary eyes to adjust. Looking off in the direction where he knew his roommate's bed to be, he said, "Xavier, are you okay?"

At first no answer then a guttural, "I said leave me alone. *Please*."

Alex wanted to press, but the plaintive tone of that *please* kept him silent. Plus Alex might play dumb, but he knew what was wrong with Xavier. He was heartbroken. He hadn't responded to Xander's message, but obviously the rejection had left him a mess.

Staggering toward his bed in the dark, Alex kept getting off course and bumping into shit. He knew he'd made it to his bed when he stubbed his toe on the frame and cursed. He stripped down to his underwear and climbed under the covers.

From the other side of the room, Xavier's voice drifted. "Dude, I think you had a few too many. I didn't even know you drank."

"Well, there's a first time for everything."

"If this is the first time you've ever been drunk, you're in for a hell of a time tomorrow."

"Guess I'm going to have one hell of a hangover."

"You're going to feel like death, and you may be praying for it before it's over. I don't envy you."

"No one envies me," Alex said. He meant it to be a joke, but it came out sounding morose and self-pitying.

Silence for a moment before Xavier responded. "I hear ya. I don't envy myself right now much either. Have you… oh, never mind."

Alex propped himself up on an elbow. "What is it? You can ask anything."

"Do you ever want something so bad, and think that it's a real possibility you're going to get it, only to have it all come crashing down around you."

Alex thought for a moment then said, "I know exactly what you mean. You know, except for the thinking it's a real possibility part."

This actually got a chuckle from Xavier. "Good night, Alex."

Alex mumbled a good night then let his head drift back to his pillow. Actually it dropped to the pillow like a bowling ball. He felt dazed, and not just from all the alcohol buzzing through his veins. This was perhaps the longest sustained conversation he and Xavier had ever had, and by far the most civil and friendly.

It seemed crazy, but what if Xander's rejection actually led Alex and Xavier to get closer, become friends, maybe even…

No, he didn't want to let his imagination carry him away. He told himself to be satisfied with just a simple conversation, a few kind words. Let that be enough.

Yet as he closed his eyes, he thought if he dreamed of a happily ever after, he couldn't fault his subconscious for the fantasy.

Sometime in the night, Xander came awake and reached for his phone. He quickly typed out a message before falling back into his slumber.

Alex dreamt that he was in the icy ocean. He had been on the Titanic but it had fallen into the sea, leaving him flailing and freezing. He could feel Death placing a glacial hand around his heart, and his limbs felt incredibly heavy. He knew he wouldn't be able to stay afloat much longer.

Then out of the darkness a lifeboat appeared. The moon shone down and spotlighted Xavier at the prow of the boat, a glowing deus ex machina. He had a hand flung out, as if reaching for Alex.

Alex swam hard, digging down deep to find his last reservoir of strength. As he drew close to the boat, a figure rose up behind Xavier. At first the figure was only a dark silhouette but then the moon caught it as well and revealed a sight that terrified Alex.

This second figure in the boat was not a person exactly, but a cartoon. A moving drawing. A drawing that Alex himself had created. Every facial contour, every curl of hair, even the mole under the left eye.

Xander, holding a paddle high over his animated head.

Alex tried to back pedal through the water to get away from the boat, but he was too late. Xander swung the paddle down in an arc, crashing into Alex's head...

Alex awoke with a start, thrashing in his covers, the pain from the paddle still reverberating in his head.

He realized a second later it had only been a dream, but the pain in his head did not recede. Then he remembered the night before, the multiple beers, and he understood the true source of the pain.

He rolled onto his side and pulled his knees up to his chest. The lights were off and the blinds closed, but enough sunlight filtered through that it made him squeeze his eyes shut against the assault. The pain in his head throbbed, pulsed, expanded, until it felt as if something had crawled into his skull to gestate and would soon break free. He thought he remembered some Greek myth about a god that was born that way, from someone's head. The agony was so intense he thought he might welcome such a birth. A shattered skull would be worth it if the pain would end.

From the bathroom, he heard the toilet flush and then Xavier came into the room. He glanced at his roommate then laughed and shook his head. "I told you this morning was going to be rough. You look like shit on a cracker."

"I feel like shit on a cracker," Alex said, his voice a hoarse croak. The effort caused another detonation in his brain.

"I'm going down to grab some breakfast at the dining hall. Don't guess you want anything, huh?"

The mere thought of food made Alex's stomach heave and churn like the freezing ocean from his dream. He shook his head slightly and instantly regretted even that minute movement.

"Well, I've been in your shoes before so here's my advice. Stay in bed, try to move as little as possible, and I put a trashcan next to your bed in case everything inside decides it wants to be outside."

"Thanks," Alex said. He wanted to be more touched that Xavier was showing him some actual concern, but he felt too bad for anything else to really penetrate.

"No problem. Now I'm going to grab some grub and then go for a jog around the lake."

Alex noticed the light tone to Xavier's voice, the permanent smile that seemed to curl his lips. "You seem like you're in a much better mood this morning than you were last night."

Xavier's smile widened even further, something Alex wouldn't have thought possible. "That's because everything's different this morning."

With that proclamation, Xavier gave him a little salute and left the dorm room.

Alex felt more than a little confused. Last night Xavier had been a heartbroken mess, and this morning he had a bounce in his step and a smile in his heart. *Everything's different this morning.* What could possibly be so different? The hangover was too intense for Alex to even entertain the fantasy that Xavier had realized after their brief conversation the previous night that Alex was his soulmate, something lame like that.

The thought struck Alex like a fist that Xavier

might be planning to go see Xander after all, show up in person to plead his case, to look Xander in the eye and ask face-to-face for a chance to see where their relationship might go.

The only problem was Xander didn't have an eye or a face.

Alex felt around for his phone, finding it stuffed under his pillow like a prize from the Tooth Fairy. He opened Snapchat, wanting to see if Xavier had finally sent a message to Xander.

And he had, a fairly lengthy one at 7:45 this morning. However, he wasn't responding to the message Alex had constructed in the laundry room, sent at 8:32 the previous evening. No, Xavier was responding to the subsequent message sent at 2:55 this morning.

If Alex hadn't felt like he was dying, he would have bolted upright in bed. Instead, he merely lay there, staring at the screen, trying to make sense of what he was seeing through the pain in his head. How could Xander have sent another message at 2:55?

The answer, of course, was that he couldn't have because Xander didn't exist. Alex had to have sent that message, and yet he had no memory of it. How was that possible?

Because you were drunk as a skunk.

Last night, after his third beer, became fuzzy, but he remembered most of it. Yet sometime after he'd crashed, he had apparently gotten back up and sent this message without any recollection of the act at all.

It seemed impossible, but Alex had heard plenty of stories of alcoholic blackouts, people doing stupid things they don't remember while under the influence. And now Alex had experienced it firsthand.

And what he'd done had been stupid indeed. He read the message three times, the words making him feel even sicker than he already did.

> Xavier, please disregard my last message. I know I can't ask you to forget it but understand that it was written from a dark place of doubt and fear and self-loathing. My ex really did a number on me making me feel like shit, like I wasn't worthy of love. I think I internalized that more than I realized. I'm scared of being hurt, yes, but more than that I'm scared that I don't deserve anything else. That's my issue, not yours. All I know is that when we chat I feel possibility. I'm not saying I'm already planning our wedding and what we'll name our adopted children but I see the possibility of opening up to someone again, being close to someone, letting someone into my heart. And that gave me a fright, let's say a PTSD reaction, and I sent that earlier message. God how I

wish I could go back in time and stop myself from sending it but what's done is done. All I can ask now is that you forgive me and understand. I do want you to come visit me. I really do. I want to see where this goes. Maybe nowhere. Maybe somewhere. But I want to find out. If you don't hate me for my previous message, I'm officially extending the invite. If not, I will understand and know I have no one to blame but myself but if you are still willing, I am still willing. I eagerly await your answer. Love your fellow X-Man."

What in the holy hell could Alex have been thinking? Even drunk, what had possessed him to extend an invite for Xavier to visit someone who didn't even exist? It was the dumbest possible move he could have made and would lead to nothing but disaster. The only explanation he could come up with was that he had been so upset by seeing Xavier so upset that his subconscious had decided to do something drastic to soothe his roommate's pain. Almost like he'd been in a sleepwalking state when he'd sent the message, dream-texting instead of drunk-texting.

He read Xavier's response, and the hope and joy in the message broke Alex's heart almost as much as Xavier's tears from the night before. More actually, because it was hope and joy built on a lie. Alex's lie.

You're forgiven! I mean there's nothing to forgive, not really. I won't lie and say I wasn't hurt. I was quite a bit actually. So much so that I even talked about it with my dweeb roommate last night. I didn't get into specifics but I definitely showed him my vulnerable side but I didn't know where else to turn. Any port in a storm as they say. I fell asleep crying but I'm not saying that to make you feel bad. I'm saying that to show you how much I do care about you, that the very idea that you might not feel the same could leave me feeling that wrecked. And when I read your message this morning, all that hurt blew away like autumn leaves.

Everything you said makes complete sense. I can understand the fear of getting close after someone has burned you. And don't ever tell me your ex's name because I'm very likely to look him up track him down and beat the ever-loving shit out of him. Just kidding. Sorta kinda maybe. I just can't imagine how anyone would be able to treat someone as wonderful as you so badly but the world is full of shitty people I suppose. I just want to assure you I would never make you feel worthless because you are worth so much to me.

I know I'm coming on strong but coming so close to losing you I feel like it's important that I let you know just how much you actually mean to me. I don't know what will happen between us but it's something I want to explore. Something I NEED to explore. So yes. Yes a million times yes, I accept your invitation! I will be there with bells on if that doesn't sound too gay. Anyway I've already Google mapped the course to the campus. I can be there bright and early Monday after next. Just tell me the time and place on campus. I can't wait to see your face."

Any port in a storm. That was what Xavier had called Alex, which meant their brief little conflab last night had meant nothing to Xavier. That stung. Fuck, it felt like a sledgehammer to the solar plexus. Then again, he mused that he had little room to feel betrayed or angry when he had concocted this ruse that was setting Xavier up for the ultimate hurt. What's worse than being rejected by someone you care about? How about finding out that person is a figment of the imagination of someone you couldn't give two shits about?

What was Alex going to do? He had a week to fix this, if it could be fixed at all. He could, of course, send yet another message saying Xander had experienced yet another change of heart, but that might leave Xavier broken. Even after being called a dweeb yet again by his roommate—though Xander had been the first one to deem him so—he still didn't want to see Xavier heartbroken. It would be so much worse the second time; after his high of this morning there was so much further to fall.

But something had to be done. Maybe a sickness? Yes, what if Xander contracted COVID? That could work, but it would need to wait until closer to time for the visit to truly be effective. Not a perfect plan, it felt a little contrived and convenient plus would be only a temporary solution, but it was better than nothing.

Any port in a storm.

Alex tossed his phone aside and rolled over, suddenly glad Xavier had left the trashcan next to the bed.

Alex spent the remainder of the day in the bathroom. Considering his hangover, Xavier didn't find this unusual. Even the suitemates next door gave him some space, not knocking on the door from their side and demanding to be let in.

Alex actually huddled fully dressed in the shower, curtain closed, feeling like he was in a tiled coffin, and watched the movie *Titanic* on his phone. The thing seemed awfully cheesy and melodramatic, but it meant something to Xavier. And since both Alex and Xander were likely to lose Xavier soon, Alex wanted something that made him feel close to his roommate. This silly old movie would have to do.

He did find some resonance in the love story. The beautiful young couple who loved each other and wanted to be together, and the cruel bastard that no one loved who tried to keep them apart. It was like Xander and Xavier were Jack and Rose, and Alex was the asshole Cal, dooming them all.

The second half of the movie, after the ship strikes the iceberg, was more exciting. Full of pain and fear and panic and senseless tragedy. That felt more realistic to Alex, a more accurate representation of life as he had experienced it.

By the end, he found himself crying. Not merely because of how the events of the film played out, but because of how the events of his own life were playing out. He was the screenwriter, director, and playing dual roles, and this film was headed for disaster. A box office flop, reviled by critics, a zero score on Rotten Tomatoes and the recipient of a bucket full of Razzies. And Alex had no one to blame but himself.

The pain in his chest felt like a balloon, expanding and ready to burst. He put the phone aside as the credits rolled, pulled his knees to his chest and rocked back and forth. He wanted to scream, to punch his fist into the mirror over the sink, go through his room like a tornado leaving destruction in his wake. But he could do none of these things; he had to keep all his hurt and rage inside, which only amplified it. He needed an outlet, something to ease the pain enough so that he could get through the day and the one after that and the one after that.

And he knew of only one thing that could give him that relief. Which was why he'd brought the scissors into the bathroom with him in the first place.

He pushed up and sat on the edge of the tub then pulled his pants down to his ankles. The scars on his thighs were fading but still visible. He had promised himself when he left for college that he was done with cutting himself, that he was going to leave the old Alex behind and recreate himself. Instead he had created Xander, an image he could never live up to, a reminder of all of Alex's own flaws and shortcomings.

With a trembling hand, he placed the tip of the scissors at the top of one of the scars then followed the line, like unzipping his own flesh. The pain was delicious, a pain to distract him from the greater pain, offering him at least a moment of peace.

Alex had trouble concentrating on his midterms and therefore suspected he was royally fucking them up. He had never been an honor roll student in high school, but his grades had been respectable. He had never actually flunked a course in his life. He feared that would change after the midterms.

He'd tried to study, but his eyes would skim the textbooks and his notes and retain no information for his brain. Then Monday when he sat for his first exam, he had to reread each question about five times to even be able to follow what was being asked. This wasn't going to end well.

Yet he had no one to blame but himself. His mind was a chaotic whirlwind of guilt and fear and recrimination. He felt a bit like he was in hell, but one of his own creation which was probably the most sadistic of hells.

Xavier and Xander had been exchanging messages, but Alex kept Xander somewhat vague when it came to plans for the visit. Xavier, for his part, seemed happy but distracted. He seemed to actually be focusing on midterm exams. However, as the week progressed, he was sure to start pressing Xander for specifics. Alex began to wonder if he could pull off the COVID excuse without it seeming like just that, an excuse? In the end, it didn't matter because it had to be done. And he had to start thinking seriously of the end game, how he was going to permanently end the burgeoning relationship between the X-Men. He thought again about the feasibility of killing off Xander.

That took up all his brain power and concentration, leaving little time for exams.

Wednesday afternoon, coming back to the room after his Psych midterm, he found Xavier packing clothes into a duffle bag.

"You leaving already?" Alex asked.

Xavier barely glanced up, stuffing some underwear in the bag. "What? Oh no, my last exam is at nine Friday morning, but I want to be ready to head out the second I'm done."

"Your parents must be excited to see you."

"I'm not headed home for break. I'm going to see a friend."

Alex threw his backpack on the bed and tried to act cool, which almost guaranteed he'd act like a freak. "What friend?"

Xavier didn't look up, but his lips spread in a euphoric smile. "Someone special. Someone *very* special."

"And you're going to see him on Friday?"

"Man, I'm not trying to be rude, but I'm kind of busy right now."

"Yeah, sure, of course. I have studying to do anyway."

Alex sat on his bed with a book open on his lap, but he didn't read anything and never actually turned the page, not that his roommate noticed. In his periphery, Alex kept a watch on Xavier as he continued to pack.

What was going on? The plan had been to drive up on Monday. If Xavier wasn't going to spend the weekend with his family, was he thinking he'd surprise Xander early? But no, he didn't know what dorm Xander lived in or anything. Perhaps the plan was to simply show up on campus then message

Xander that he was there.

When Xavier went to the bathroom, Alex snatched up his phone to see if Xavier had sent any messages to Xander since this morning. He was surprised to find he was logged out of his Snapchat. And when he entered his log-in information, it told him that the information entered was invalid. He tried again, then again, but still couldn't get logged in. He tried to reset that password, but it said the email address he entered was no longer the one associated with the account.

Which was impossible. Somehow he had gotten locked out of Xander's Snapchat, but how could the email address have been changed? It didn't make sense. Unless his account had been hacked.

The thought terrified him. Who would have hacked into the account, and for what purpose? Did someone know what he was doing to Xavier—the gaslighting, the catfishing—and were they planning to use that information against him?

When Xavier came back in from the bathroom, Alex stuffed his phone and book into his backpack and said he was going to study in the library. Xavier didn't even acknowledge him as he left. Instead of going to the library, however, Alex went down to the lake and sat down on a bench looking out toward the bell tower.

He tried again, unsuccessfully, to get into the Snapchat account. He had no idea what was going on, but perhaps he could view this as a blessing. He then got on Instagram and saw that he now only had one account, his original account. The second Xander account had been deactivated.

"What the fuck is going on?" Alex said, perhaps too loudly but there was no one around but the ducks to hear him.

Had whoever hacked Snapchat also hacked his Instagram? If so, that meant he was targeted by someone. He quickly made a new Snapchat account and then searched for Xander's. He found it, but the account had been made private.

Alex gripped the phone, trying to figure out what to do. He could access nothing that belonged to the Xander persona.

This was troubling, to say the least, but in a weird way it also felt like a relief. If he had lost access to Xander then he could no longer trade communications with Xavier. It was out of his hands now.

And maybe that was for the best.

Alex almost skipped his exams on Thursday. In the end, he went but thought he might as well not have. He knew he had to have failed them miserably. Could it have been any worse if he simply hadn't taken them? He couldn't stop thinking about the hack of the Xander social media accounts.

Yes, on one level it made things easier for Alex, lifted a weight from his shoulders, but that was only if he didn't think too deeply about it. There was still the question of who had done this and why. That kept him on edge, waiting for the other shoe to drop.

That night as he sat at his desk, he contemplated contacting Snapchat and Instagram, telling them his accounts had been hacked and seeing if he could get control of them back. But he also wondered if he could get in trouble for posing as someone else. Surely not, other people did it all the time. Right?

He wasn't sure and it kept him from reporting the hacks.

Behind him, he heard Xavier laugh. Glancing over his shoulder, he saw his roommate reclined on his bed, scrolling on his phone. He hadn't seemed particularly upset, even though he couldn't have heard from Xander all day.

"What are you doing?" Alex asked.

"Messaging with a friend."

"One of the guys from the lacrosse team?"

"No," Xavier said, laughing again at something on his screen. "It's my friend I'm going to visit for fall break."

"What?" Alex said, standing so abruptly it sent his chair toppling over.

Xavier put down his phone and sat up on the bed, looking at Alex as if he'd gone crazy. "What the fuck is wrong with you, dude?"

Alex didn't know what to say, but a million thoughts were going through his mind. If Xavier was messaging with Xander, that meant whoever had hacked into the accounts was actually posing as Xander. Someone had taken Alex's mask and put it on as their own?

But why? What game was afoot?

"You're being a total freak right now," Xavier said when Alex continued to stand rigidly by his desk, saying nothing.

"It's just that… " Alex trailed off, not sure how to finish that sentence. Should he tell Xavier now, come clean, so he would know that someone was trying to trick him.

The way Alex had already been tricking him. Perhaps this was the mysterious hacker's plan, to force Alex to confess.

"I'm out of here," Xavier said, getting up from the bed and putting on his shoes. "Just when I start to think you're at least semi-quasi-normal, you prove to me what a weirdo you really are."

Alex watched him go, unable to say anything, but a dread settling over him like a wet blanket.

Alex lay in bed, trying to keep his breathing evened out, pretending to sleep while he waited for his roommate to go to sleep. Xavier didn't come back to the room until almost midnight, but he said nothing to Alex, simply went into the bathroom to change into his pajamas and then crawled into his bed. But he stayed up on his phone for another hour.

And only when Xavier's breathing became even and stayed that way for another hour did Alex feel confident to creep out of his own bed and across the room. Xavier always kept his cell charging on his nightstand, and that was where Alex found it now.

Unplugging the phone and scampering away on his tiptoes, he locked himself in the bathroom, feeling like some kind of criminal.

He prayed the screen wouldn't be locked, but like most prayers, this one was not answered. He cursed softly, feeling tears threatening to rain down. How in the world could he figure out the passcode for Xavier's phone? He knew his roommate's birthday was December 11th, so he tried 1211 but that wasn't it. He was almost ready to go back into the room and put the phone back when an idea struck him.

During all the conversations between Xavier and Xander, Alex had given Xander quite the backstory and bio, including a birthday. Alex sat on the edge of the tub and had to think a minute before it came to him. July 5th. That was it, because Xavier had made the joke that if he'd been born just a day earlier he could have been called Yankee Doodle Xander.

With trembling fingers, Alex typed in 0605. That couldn't be it, surely that wasn't it, that would be too simple for…

Alex stared down at the screen for almost a full

moment before his brain could accept that he'd succeeded and was now staring at the home screen. The wallpaper was one of Xander's drawings, the "self-portrait" used as his Instagram profile pic. Xander's birthday as his passcode, his picture as his wallpaper. Xavier had fallen hard for Xander, no doubt about that.

Alex opened up Snapchat and went to the messages. He actually gasped when he saw how many messages had been exchanged between Xavier and Xander since Alex had been locked out of the account. He had to scroll back for quite a while.

Whoever was impersonating Xander—which was supposed to be Alex's job—had suggested Xavier not wait until Monday but come up for the weekend too. Xavier loved that idea, and the two proceeded to make plans. Xavier would leave right after his last exam on Friday, and he should reach Xander's school by four that afternoon if he drove straight through. They would meet at the campus coffee shop for awkward introductions and caffeine. Xavier asked where he should stay, if there were any reasonable motels nearby, an intentionally obvious ploy that worked when Xander said his roommate had dropped out so he had a free bed in his dorm room.

The chats got more flirtatious than suggestive. Xander talked about different things they could do around town, places he could show Xavier, and when Xavier responded:

If we leave the room at all that is...

Xander only sent back the devil head emoji.

The chats were so elaborate, whoever had hacked into the Xander account had obviously read through the previous ones because he kept the backstory Alex had created straight and even built on it. Alex couldn't believe what he was reading.

But the final shock came at the end. Xander finally sent Xavier a photo. Not a drawing, not a sketch, but an honest-to-god photo.

And he looked exactly like Alex's "Ideal" drawing.

Which was impossible. Alex hadn't based that drawing on a real person, instead taking features from different actors and models and stitching them together Frankenstein-style. How could the hacker have found a photo of someone who looked exactly like the drawing, every feature and contour?

Alex closed the app and crept back into the room, returning his roommate's phone and plugging it up. After crawling back under the covers, he lay wide awake, knowing sleep was an impossibility. The mystery had just gotten deeper and weirder and Alex didn't know what to do.

Alex dreamt that Xavier and Xander had teamed up to fight crime, both of them wearing ridiculously tight and brightly colored leotards that showed off their rippling muscles underneath. Bold X's were emblazoned on their chests. The X-Men.

They flew around, just below the clouds, holding hands as they dipped and dove and laughed. They scanned the earth for those in need of saving. At one point they caught a girl mid-fall from a cliff, then tore off the roof of a car to free someone who was trapped inside after crashing into a ravine. They even rescued a scared kitten from the roof of a house. Everywhere they went, people cheered and applauded these two who embodied everything manly and confident and strong.

Then they spotted someone tying a damsel to railroad tracks. In the distance, the sound of an approaching train could be heard. Xavier and Xander exchanged a mid-air glance, nodded at one another, then plummeted down.

They snatched the man up and whirled him around. It was Alex himself. He was the bad guy. Dressed all in black, his hair slicked back, he laughed in the faces of the X-Men. "You meddling fools, you can't stop me."

"We're not here to stop you," Xavier said then threw Alex into a ladder-back kitchen chair that had materialized out of nowhere. The two X-Men proceeded to tie Alex securely to the chair.

On the railroad tracks, the damsel shouted for help as the train screamed ever closer. She thrashed against her own restraints but could not get free. Watching, Alex felt suddenly uncomfortable. Yes, he had put her there, but the story was supposed to go that the heroes would arrive in the nick of time and save her. However, the X-Men merely stood off to the side, arms folded, and watched as well.

"What are you doing?" Alex said, raising his voice to be heard over the train. "Why aren't you saving her?"

Xander glanced over, his impossibly beautiful face like stone. "We didn't come here to save him."

"Him?" Alex said then looked back toward the tracks. He had been mistaken; that was no damsel tied to the tracks. No, he saw himself. Alex had tied himself to the tracks to be flattened by the train.

As the Alex on the tracks fought in vain against his ropes, the Alex in the chair did the same. Their voices melded together as they shouted in unison. "Do something! Save me!"

The X-Men laughed and Xander turned to him. "We couldn't save you even if we wanted to, which we don't. You were the only one who could have saved yourself, but instead you tied yourself to those tracks. You brought this on yourself."

Alex was crying, both of him. "Then why did you come here if you weren't going to save me?"

Xavier answered, his lips twisted up in a sadistic smile. "To make sure you watched your own destruction."

Both versions of Alex screamed up at the sky as the train came and—

Alex awoke with a shudder and a sick groan. A glance at the clock told him it was 4:25 a.m. He was surprised he'd gotten any sleep at all, but he didn't feel remotely rested. Not after that dream. He lay in bed for another fifteen minutes, listening to the sound of Xavier's light snores across the room. Yet quiet as it was, his head was filled with so much noise. Noise that sounded like a train bearing down on him. Finally, accepting that there would be no more sleep, he slipped out of bed. He couldn't lay there staring into the darkness any longer. He had to act.

He couldn't say he'd devised anything close to a plan, but he had the beginnings of a strategy. A next step, at least.

He dressed quietly in the dark, being careful not to wake Xavier, then crept out of the room. At this hour, the dorm was eerily silent, the only sound the soft crooning of a radio on an upper floor. Perhaps someone pulling an all-night cram session for exams.

Alex had two exams scheduled for today, but he wouldn't be taking either of them. He wouldn't think of the consequences of skipping out on the midterms, at least not now. He had other things on his mind which in the moment felt much more important.

Once out of the dorm, he made his way to the parking lot, the sodium vapor lamps casting little yellow pools of light onto the pavement like puddles of piss. His car was parked near the back end of the lot. An old Pontiac that had once belonged to his mother. It wasn't the best looking car, dented and scratched and missing the passenger's side mirror, but it got him around where he needed to be.

Of course, the trip he was about to take was further than just a quick jaunt downtown, but he would have to hope the vehicle was up to the task. What other choice did he have?

Behind the wheel, he didn't crank the car right away. Instead, he plugged his phone into the charger and quickly went through the steps to create a new Snapchat account. He immediately looked up Xander and sent a message.

> I don't know who you are but I suspect you know exactly who I am. I don't know what you think you're doing or what your plan is but I'm begging you to leave Xavier out of it. If you've got a problem, it's with me not with him. It may sound rich coming from me but he doesn't deserve to be messed with anymore. I know I'm the one that started this but it needs to end now. Whatever your end game is, don't punish Xavier for my stupidity.

After sending the message, he turned the key, listened to the car chugging and sputtering as he backed out of the spot and followed the dim headlights out of the lot and onto the road.

The drive was lonely and quiet. He could have turned on some music, but he decided to stay locked up in the car with only his thoughts for company. He still didn't have a concrete plan, and was running purely on instinct and insanity. As the sun came up, first just a blazing line on the horizon before bleeding out to infect the entire sky and chase away the stars, Alex felt the exhaustion settling into his bones, weighing down his eyelids. He pulled into a fast food drive through for a large cup of steaming coffee. The caffeine gave him a much needed jolt, even if the coffee tasted like the bottom of an ashtray.

He kept checking his phone to see if he had a reply from the Xander Snapchat account. So far nothing, though the sent icon was hollow which meant it had been opened. So whoever the hacker was, they had seen the message and were choosing not to respond.

Halfway through the trip, Alex's stomach began to rumble and he realized he should have gotten a breakfast biscuit or something when he stopped for the coffee, but he didn't want to stop again. He should have time, he was far ahead of Xavier, but he didn't want to risk it. Plus he had this superstitious fear that the Pontiac would keep running as long as he kept the forward momentum going, but any extra stops would increase the likelihood it would conk out on him.

He did have to stop for gas once, but he kept the car running as he filled up even though he'd always heard that was dangerous. He took the opportunity to run inside the gas station and grab a big bag of Doritos and a Mountain Dew. Breakfast of champions and idiots.

He pulled up to the college at half-past noon, driving around the periphery for a while before finding a visitor's lot and parking the car. Still no response from the imposter Xander.

You're the imposter Xander, a voice in Alex's head reminded him. *At least originally.*

Okay, so he had still received no response from the *new* imposter Xander. The imposter imposter. Alex knew that two wrongs didn't make a right, but what did two imposters make?

He shook his head, as if trying to dislodge this string of thought that was starting to feel increasingly more unhinged.

He still had several hours to wait until the proposed meeting between Xavier and Xander, and knowing of nothing else to do, he got out of the car and began to wander around the campus. This school was much larger than Alex's, and he found the layout a little confusing. He pulled up the school's website on his phone and downloaded a map, but he'd never had the kind of brain that could really follow all those little lines and icons and legends. With the map he felt even more lost.

The campus was full of kids, walking and skateboarding and biking and even razor-scootering from building to building. None of them paid him much attention. To them, he probably looked like just another student they didn't know. In fact, any number of the people he passed could have been pretending to be someone else like he was. Maybe everybody was pretending, and no one could tell from the outside.

Alex took a seat on a bench next to a bike path and searched the map for the only place that mattered to him. The campus café. Unlike at his school where the café was part of the bookstore, here they were separate. The café appeared to be almost smack-dab in the middle of campus, next to the administration building. Now Alex simply had to figure out where he was currently.

The nearest building had a sign out front identifying it as the library. He zoomed in and found that on the map then tried to trace a route to the café. It looked fairly simple, but he still took a few minutes deciding in which direction he needed to go from here. Then by constantly checking the building names against the map, he eventually found himself standing outside the café.

The place was packed, the crowd spilling out to nearby picnic tables. He thought about getting a frappe, but he didn't feel up to waiting in that line and being surrounded by all those people. He did scan the crowd, though he wasn't sure what he was looking for. The face from the photo sent to Xavier, Alex's drawing come to life? A cartoon villain with a twirly mustache and a black hat?

All he saw were college students, laughing and talking, lost in their phones and tablets, playing the socializing game. A game Alex had never been good at, could never figure out the rules.

He wandered around, looking for the perfect place to covertly watch the bookstore's entrance. The perfect place that would offer a good view while keeping him hidden from Xavier when he showed up.

The perfect place to spy.

He found an old wooden bench that seemed forgotten, half hidden under the overhanging branches of a weeping willow. Names and curse words had been carved into the wood, which was buckling and splintering, but he didn't mind the discomfort. He sat down and waited.

As Alex waited, he ran through different possible scenarios of what was going to happen at four o'clock. Xavier would show up and some stranger would approach him; Xavier would show up and someone who looked vaguely like the Xander drawing would approach him; Xavier would show up and no one would approach him and he'd think himself stood up.

None of these scenarios made much sense. Whoever the hacker was, Alex couldn't fathom the motivation behind this deception. And even more than that, Alex couldn't fathom what he would do in any of these situations. Confrontation seemed a recipe for disaster no matter what happened, so why had he driven all this way? Merely to observe?

He might as well have brought a bag of popcorn

so he could munch while he watched the story unfold. A story he had started, but like a screenwriter who loses control of a project and his script gets rewritten by nameless others, Alex had no idea how this was going to end. And he couldn't decide his next move until he knew what the hacker would do next.

Time crept by, as if the world had slowed its spinning. The day was bright but cool, the first hint of autumn on the breeze. The leaves had only started to change, reds and oranges creeping into the greenery. A textbook beautiful day, but Alex barely noticed. It could have been gray and storming, frigid and snowing, it wouldn't have made a difference to him. He thought about getting up and wandering the campus some more, but he didn't want to give up his hiding spot. He watched as kids came and went at the café like actors on a stage, Alex waiting for a specific performance.

At 3:40, he perked up when he saw Xavier approaching the café. He made good time. Either he rushed through his exam or drove well above any posted speed limits to get here. For a moment, Alex wondered if his roommate had parked in the same lot and worried he might recognize Alex's car. Then he realized that as far as he knew, Xavier had no idea what kind of car Alex drove.

Xavier got in line at the café, bought a drink of some kind, then took a seat at an empty picnic table outside. Almost as if orchestrated, Alex had the perfect vantage spot to observe his roommate sipping at the drink, checking his phone, drumming his fingers nervously on the tabletop. Alex could even see Xavier's leg jittering under the table. Alex had never seen Xavier so nervous, but why shouldn't he be? This was basically a first date as far as he knew.

Alex realized distantly that he needed to pee, but he couldn't risk leaving his spot now, not when he was so close to what he came here for. Besides, the nearest restroom was in the café itself, and he couldn't go inside without walking right past his roommate. He merely crossed his legs and waited to see who, if anyone, would show up.

Xavier saw him first. He stood up from the table and held up a hand, his lips spreading in a smile. Alex followed his roommate's gaze, and what he saw left him feeling as if the world had gone insane. Or he had.

The young man approaching Xavier with a matching smile was, like the photograph, the exact personification of Alex's "Ideal" drawing. This wasn't someone with a passing resemblance; this was Alex's drawing come to life. This was Xander, striding confidently over to Xavier. The two men hesitated for just a moment then broke the awkwardness with a hug. Not one of those half-assed hugs that straight guys sometimes gave each other, but a full-body embrace that lasted almost a full minute.

Xavier gestured toward the café entrance and said something Alex couldn't hear, Xander shook his head and said something back then the two took a seat. Alex could imagine the exchange. Xavier: You want to grab a drink? Xander: I'm fine, let's just sit and talk.

Although at first they didn't do much but sit and stare at each other in silence.

Alex felt inexplicably hot despite the cool breeze, sweat starting to form at his hairline and trickle down his face. His breathing came in pants, as if he had just finished a jog, and he blinked rapidly several times as if the sight of Xander was just a mote in his eye he could clear.

He considered again the very real possibility that he may have lost his mind. Was he merely hallucinating Xander over there? But Xavier was there too. Unless he wasn't. Could Alex also be hallucinating his roommate? Was Alex in college at all, or was he in some psych ward somewhere and this whole thing existed solely in his head?

Alex shook his head again. He didn't have time to go down this rabbit hole. He had no explanation for what he was seeing right now, but if he watched anymore he feared he might throw up or faint.

He got up from the bench and hurried around the tree and across the quad, putting as much distance between himself and the café as he could. He stopped in a random classroom building to relieve his aching bladder, then wandered around the campus for almost an hour looking for the lot where he'd parked his car. He could have pulled up the map again, but he needed time to clear his head.

And that was exactly what it felt like, as if his mind had been emptied of all coherent thought until it was an empty vessel, a pitcher with all the liquid poured out. What was happening seemed too big, too bizarre, too impossible for him to comprehend so he didn't even try. Instead, his brain seemed to shut down and he moved like a zombie through campus.

When he found the visitor's lot he'd parked in, it was almost as if he stumbled across it by accident. He climbed inside the car and wasn't at all surprised when it didn't crank. He turned the key a few times, eliciting just a whining sound under the hood, and then let his hand drop away. He sat behind the wheel and let the minutes tick away. He didn't get out of the car, he didn't pull out his phone to look up towing services or mechanics in the area. He merely sat there, staring out the windshield, feeling numbed and hollow.

He didn't even react when the passenger's door opened and someone climbed inside the car. It was almost as if he had been waiting for it.

Alex didn't turn his head, not wanting to look directly at his not-entirely unexpected visitor. He kept his gaze trained straight ahead. He could make out a bit of the person's shape in his periphery, the curly hair and broad shoulders, but a part of him felt like to face this person and meet eye to eye would be like staring into the sun. It could lead only to blindness.

Or madness.

"I figured you'd show up here," the person said, and though the deep voice wasn't familiar to Alex, on some level it was. It was the voice he always imagined when typing out the messages to Xavier.

Alex tried to speak, only managed a hoarse croak, coughed and licked his lips then tried again. "Who are you?"

"Xander, but you already know that. I mean, in a way you're my father."

Alex shook his head. "That's impossible. Xander isn't real."

"I wasn't, but then neither were you before you were born."

"Xander isn't real," Alex said again. "*I'm* Xander."

The laugh that came from beside him was full and loud. "Now we both know that isn't true. Xander is fun and interesting, athletic and active, he has a great sense of humor and lots of friends. Does any of that sound remotely like *you*?"

"I don't understand. How can any of this be happening?"

"If you're looking for explanations, I'm not your guy. I didn't ask for this life, but now that I have it I plan to make the most of it. If I had to venture a guess, I'd say that you wanted to create a man who was everything you wished you could be but knew you could never be, and you wanted it hard enough and strong enough and desperately enough that you made it happen. Then you tried to get rid of me, even contemplated killing me off, and I think that was when I started to assert my own will. Call it the survival instinct kicking in."

Alex felt tears dribbling down his cheeks, but he made no move to wipe them away. He honestly wasn't sure he could move at all. "What do you want from me?"

"Nothing," Xander said. "I mean, other than creating me you have absolutely nothing I want or need. Now if I could just get rid of the umbilical."

"Umbilical?"

"Yeah. It's like, I can block you on social media, but the fact is there's this invisible tether that joins us. I can feel it, that's why I knew you were coming here. Right now even through your daze, I can feel your confusion and your horror and the self-loathing that is ever-present. Do you have any idea what it's like just trying to get through the day while feeling what it's like to be you? Hell, even *you* don't want to be *you*. This situation is not sustainable, so one of us has to go."

"Go?" Alex said, and the word came out like a sob.

"Well, it shouldn't be me. I mean, of the two of us, I'm the only one with any kind of real life. Sort of ironic when you think about it, but it's also true. You sleepwalk through life, have no real connections, not even with your family. I'm the one with friends and ambitions and potential. I'm the one who is actually *living*. So why don't you cut the cord and let me really live?"

"What are you – "

"I know about the scars on your thighs, the little hatch-marks counting out all your pains big and small. And I know there are a few fresh cuts under your pants as well. I can feel them burning and pulsing. Seems to me you've been working up to this moment for years, you've only lacked the nerve to stop beating around the bush and dive in. I know those are mixed-metaphors, but you get the point."

"You want me to… ? No, no, that's insane."

In his periphery, Alex saw Xander lean toward him and when he spoke, he'd lowered his voice to almost a whisper. "Would you really miss this life? Would anyone in it miss you? Why don't you clear the field and make room for someone who will appreciate the life he was given, really do something with it? A noble sacrifice, wouldn't you say?"

Alex didn't answer, but his tears came heavier, blurring the view out the windshield.

"Think about it," Xander said, reaching over and patting Alex on the thigh. "I have to go, Xavier is waiting for me. But I'm leaving you a little gift."

After the passenger's door opened and closed, Alex remained still for several minutes until the tears finally dried up. Glancing over at the empty seat, he saw that it wasn't entirely empty after all. A pocket knife with the blade extended had been left behind. With a shaking hand, Alex reached over and picked up the knife, staring at his distorted reflection in the shining surface. He barely recognized himself, the eyes staring back at him like those of a stranger.

Or a ghost.

Like Xander, Alex could feel his cuts throbbing beneath the material of his jeans. He fantasized about slicing open his flesh, but not on his legs this time.

Not straight across. It's more effective to go down from wrist to elbow.

Alex squeezed his eyes closed, trying to shut off the voice in his head that sounded just like Xander, but it would not be silenced. Everything about this situation was crazy, and he didn't know what was real and what wasn't, but regardless if this were truly happening or the product of a diseased mind, he supposed it all came down to one simple choice.

As autumn leaves swirled around the car, he sat there staring at the knife, trying to work up the nerve.

The nerve to live or the nerve to die?

That was the choice.

Mark Allan Gunnells loves to tell stories. He has since he was a kid, penning one-page tales that were Twilight Zone knockoffs. He likes to think he has gotten a little better since then. He loves reader feedback, and above all he loves telling stories. He lives in Greer, SC, with his husband Craig A. Metcalf.